Brown Rabbit's Day

Alan Baker

A BUNNY'S COOKBOOK

101 WAYS TO COOK A CARROT

RAPID RADISH RECIPES

BREAKFAST FOR BUNNIES

THE SLIMMER RABBIT COOKBOOK

JUST DESSERTS!

Kingfisher

NEW YORK

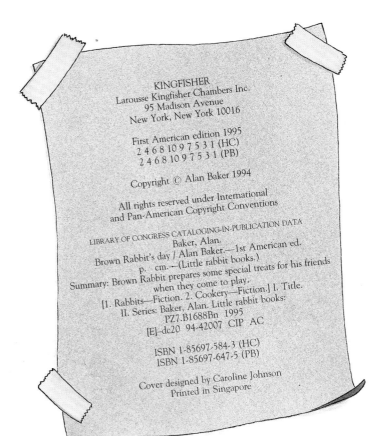

KINGFISHER
Larousse Kingfisher Chambers Inc.
95 Madison Avenue
New York, New York 10016

First American edition 1995
2 4 6 8 10 9 7 5 3 1 (HC)
2 4 6 8 10 9 7 5 3 1 (PB)

LIBRARY OF CONGRESS CATALOGING-IN-PUBLICATION DATA
Baker, Alan.
Brown Rabbit's day / Alan Baker.—1st American ed.
p.   cm.—(Little rabbit books.)
Summary: Brown Rabbit prepares some special treats for his friends
when they come to play.
[1. Rabbits—Fiction. 2. Cookery—Fiction.] I. Title.
II. Series: Baker, Alan. Little rabbit books.
PZ7.B1688Bn 1995
[E]–dc20 94-42007 CIP AC

ISBN 1-85697-584-3 (HC)
ISBN 1-85697-647-5 (PB)

Cover designed by Caroline Johnson
Printed in Singapore

Early one morning,
Brown Rabbit found
his favorite recipe book
beside his bed.
It gave him a good idea.

VEGETABLE COOKING FOR ONE

CTTUCE EAT!

MINUTES

RTAINING
GREENS

BEANS FOR BEGINNERS

At breakfast time
he wrote notes
to his friends.

After breakfast
he found some
Jell-O molds.

Then slowly and carefully he made four batches.
First, a plum purple Jell-O.
Second, a dandelion yellow Jell-O.
Third, a lettuce green Jell-O.
Last, a radish red Jell-O.

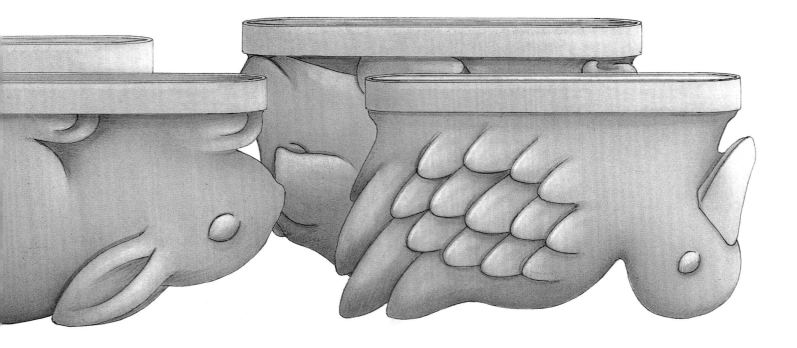

Brown Rabbit left the Jell-O to set and went to fetch strawberries, radishes, dandelion flowers, and other good things to eat.

He kept testing the Jell-O
to see if it was ready.
Hurry up, Jell-O!
he thought.

At lunchtime Brown Rabbit
ate a big juicy apple.

Then he tested the molds again. At last
they were set. Brown Rabbit carefully
turned them out. A plum purple pig.
A dandelion yellow duck. A lettuce
green hen and a radish red rabbit.

They looked delicious!

Brown Rabbit
decorated them
with fruit
and vegetables.

He was just finishing
the final decorations
when...

...his friends
arrived
to play.

First they played hopping.
Watch out, Brown Rabbit!

Then they played leaping.

Be careful with your paws, Brown Rabbit!
All afternoon they played until...

...it was time to eat the Jell-O.
Jell-O with dandelion flowers, Jell-O

with strawberries, Jell-O with radishes, and Jell-O with lettuce. Delicious!

Thank you, Brown Rabbit,
said his friends sleepily
as they waved
good-bye.

How fast time goes when
you're having fun,
he thought.

What a busy day.
Goodnight, Brown Rabbit!